JOB SITE

Nathan Clement

BOYDS MILLS PRESS
Honesdale, Pennsylvania

Boss says, "Level that pile!"

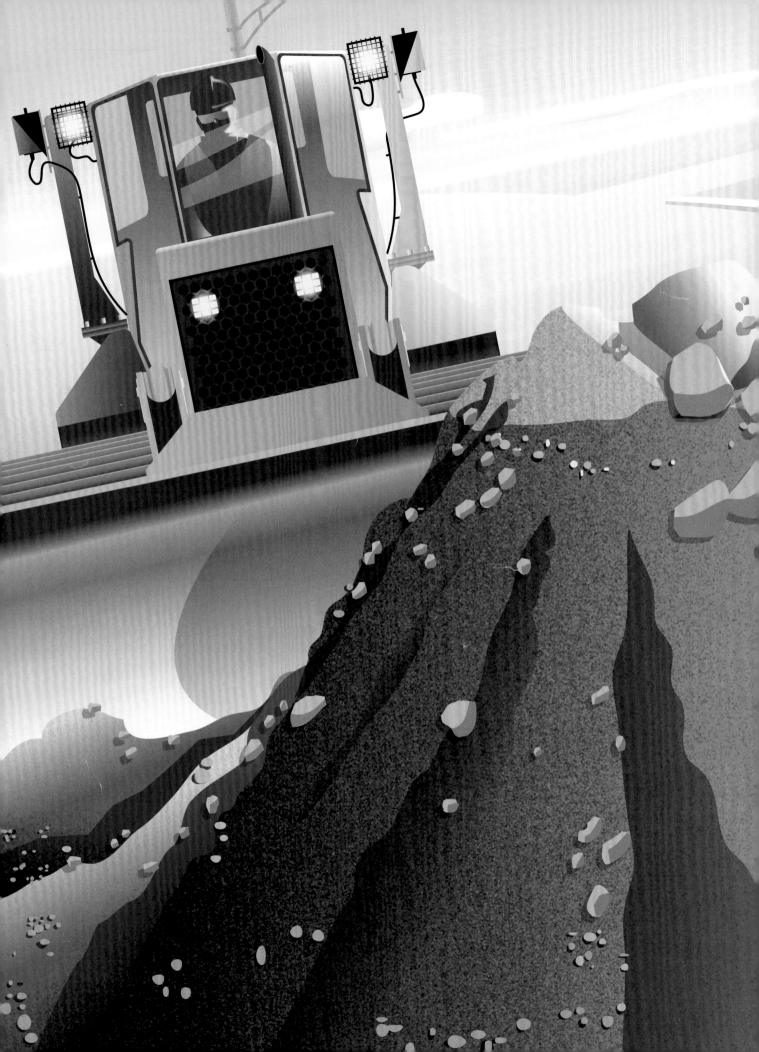

And the bulldozer lowers its blade
and levels the pile of gravel.

Boss says, "Dig a hole!"

And the excavator tips its bucket
and starts to dig.

Boss says, "Scoop that rock."

And the loader slides its bucket
and takes a big scoop.

Boss says, "Dump some gravel here."

And the dump truck lifts its bed
and dumps its gravel.

Boss says, "Pack down that spot!"

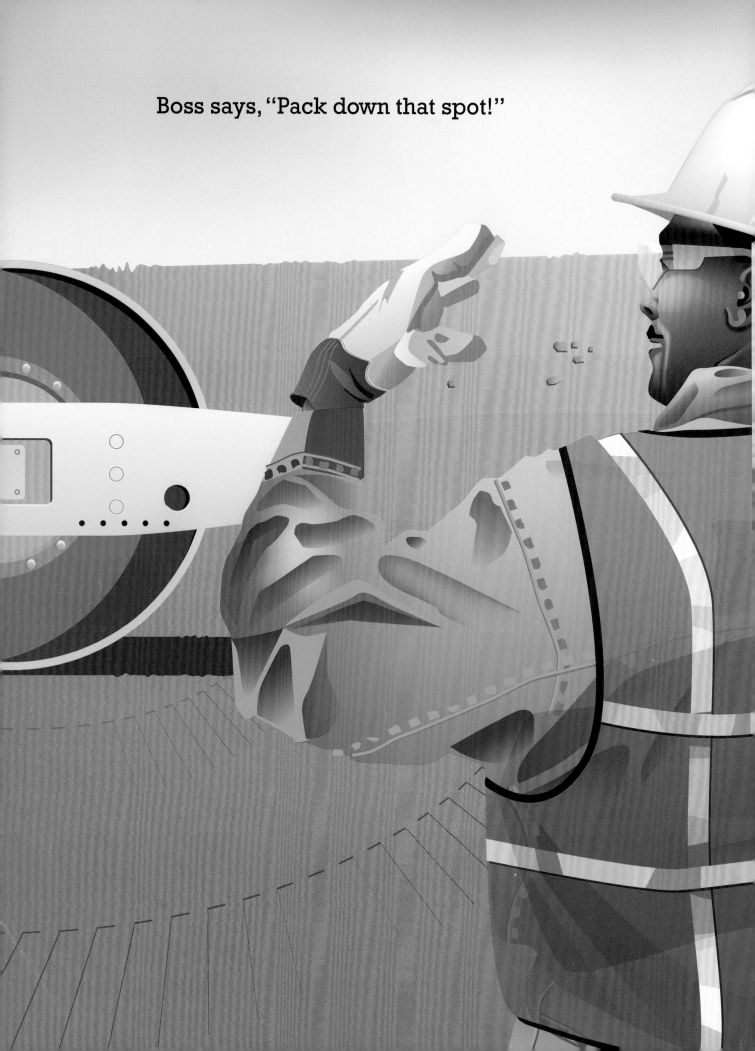

And the compactor rolls
and packs the ground firm.

Boss says, "Pour a slab."

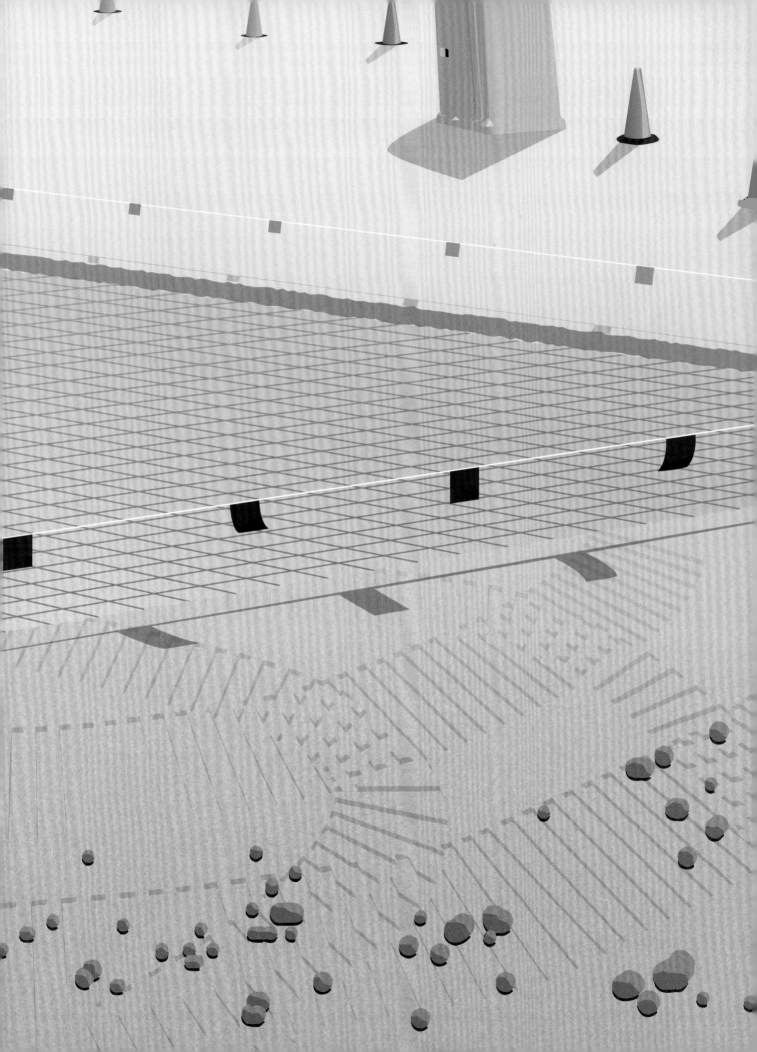

And the mixer swings its trough
and pours cement.

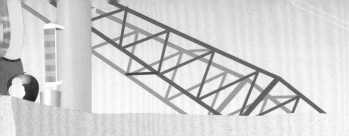

Boss says, "Lift that stone!"

And the crane lifts the stone into place.

Finally, Boss says, "This job is done!"

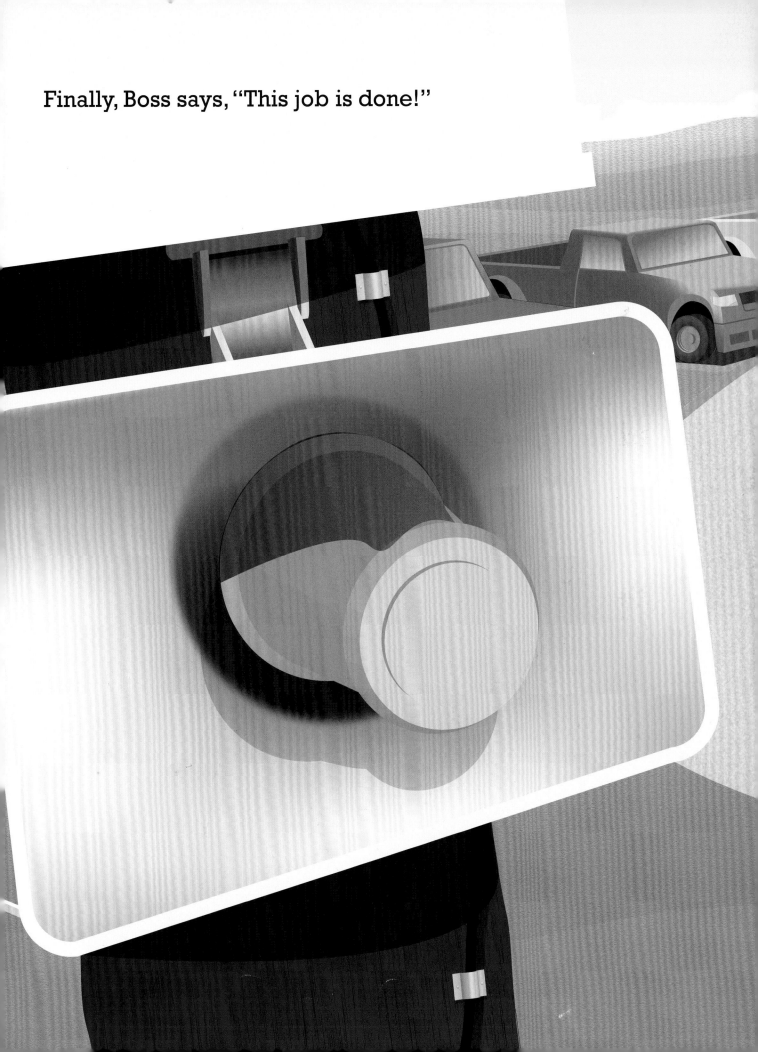

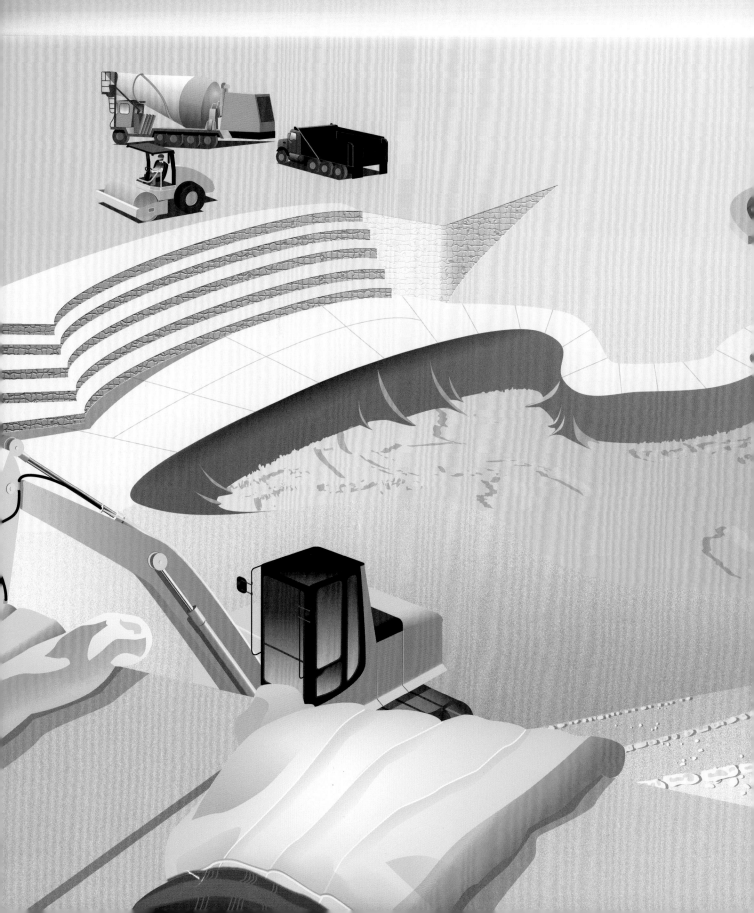

And the bulldozer, excavator, loader,
dump truck, compactor, mixer, and crane
roll away to the next job site.

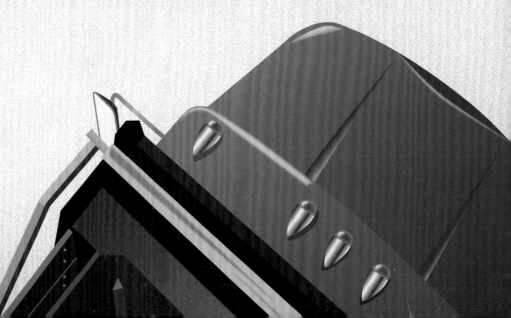

Thanks to Bob Johnson for lending years of construction expertise.
Thanks to Kevin McMichael for being a great "Boss."

Boyds Mills Press, Inc.
815 Church Street
Honesdale, Pennsylvania 18431
Printed in the United States of America

ISBN: 978-1-59078-769-4

Library of Congress Control Number: 2010929542

First edition
The text of this book is set in 18-point Rockwell.
The pictures in this book are computer rendered. Just as an artist may use
oil paint, Nathan uses color fills and blends within shapes to create his
artwork. Everything he makes begins as pencil drawings before the
computer magic can ever happen.

10 9 8 7 6 5 4 3 2